"Nadia, I can't go down there without the rest of the family," Maryam cried. "You call 911. I will crawl down the hall. Don't worry!"

Nadia watched as the image of her sister crawling faded into the smoke and flames. She did not have a good feeling about this, but she knew that there was not much she could say or do to convince Maryam to come with her.

"Come on Eppa," she said soothingly to her screaming little sister.

The two got down the stairs fairly easy. However, when they reached the bottom, Nadia was horrified to see that the entire front half of the store had already burned. There was no way she could get to the telephone!

She felt like panicking, but she knew from her emergency training in Iraq that panicking would not help. She knew that instead, she had to keep her head cool if there was any chance to save herself and her family.

FROM DESERT TO DETROIT

To my friends at Curves,
Happy reading!

Written by Donna Gundle-Krieg
Donna Gundle-Krieg

Blitz Krieg Publishing Company
Milford, Michigan
www.blitzkriegpublishing.com

ISBN 1-59113-532-X

Printed in the United States of America.

Blitz Krieg Publishing Company
Milford, Michigan
www.blitzkriegpublishing.com

FROM DESERT TO DETROIT

By Donna Gundle-Krieg

*This book is dedicated
to those who treat others
as they would like to be treated
themselves.*

Acknowledgements

This book has been a work in process for several years, and was written when I found time between "real work," fun, chores, errands, friends and family (not necessarily in that order!)

I'm grateful that my friends and family have been so supportive, especially my husband Dennis. He comes home from a long day at work to do laundry, help cook meals and drive kids around so that I can find time to write. His attention to detail also qualifies him to be my primary proofreader!

Thanks also to my creative and wonderful children, Steven and Elizabeth. Both of them have read this book many times, and didn't hesitate to tell me which parts they liked, as well as which parts were boring or confusing to their young minds. My original inspiration for this book was Elizabeth's love for her ethnically diverse group of dolls and the historical tales that went with them.

Thanks to my mother Jeannine, whose wonderful faith and spirit helped her manage a remarkable recovery from a stroke a few years ago. She has taught me to smile and keep plugging away, no matter what.

Thanks to my father Don, who died while I was still revising this book. As a businessman, he never understood why I would want to be a writer. Yet he always taught me to aggressively follow my dreams.

Thanks to Mary Burck, a truly creative artist and good friend, who came up with the idea for the front book cover.

To Angela of Booklocker.com and Julie of Jules Avenue Graphics: thanks for patiently answering my many questions regarding the publishing of my first book.

A huge thanks goes to the Saroki family, especially my best friend Pauline and her sister Marsha, who agreed to let me use one of her old school pictures for the cover.

The Sarokis are Chaldean and have been my good friends for over 30 years. Many of the ideas for this book came from the years I spent working at their family stores and hanging around their family home.

The final and most important thanks go to God the Father, his Son Jesus, and the Holy Spirit. They gave me everything I have, including my talents. By publishing this book, I am giving these talents back.

TABLE OF CONTENTS

Chapter 1
The New Swimming Pool

"How could there be so many rich people in America?" Nadia Sefro thought to herself. She looked out the window as her father drove slowly by the huge new houses that resembled castles.

How she wished she lived in the suburban cities like her cousins! She knew she would never get bored if she had so much house and yard to explore.

Nadia sighed sadly as her thoughts turned from the big houses back to her own family's small apartment on top of their party store in the middle of Detroit.

The apartment was not nearly big enough for the seven people who lived there. Not only did she have to share a room with her two sisters, there was constant arguing over the one bathroom that the entire family had to share.

Nadia's mother must have known what Nadia was thinking. "Now children, don't forget how much more we have than some of your cousins who are still in Iraq," she said.

"Remember how small our house was in Iraq? Here in America, we have our own business which allows us to eat and have a safe place to live."

The five children mockingly joined in harmony as Mrs. Sefro finished her familiar speech. "How blessed we are to live in a country where there is no war!"

Nadia knew that her mother was right, but she couldn't resist stealing a glance at Maryam and Adam, her older sister and brother. Maryam winked at Nadia and rolled her eyes, just like Nadia knew that she would. Adam had his hand over his mouth as if to stifle a chuckle.

Maryam and Adam both occasionally made fun of their parents, but neither ever complained because they were old enough to remember the old country and all the problems there.

Even though four of the Sefro children remembered the horrors in Iraq, the older two still half wished they were still back there. Nadia felt very sorry for Adam and Maryam. She knew that they had a hard time adjusting to their new life in America, and that they missed many of their friends who were left behind in Iraq. She also knew that neither one of them had made many new friends at the huge schools they attended in Detroit.

It was hardest on her sister Maryam. She was about 15, though no one in the Sefro family was sure of his or her exact age. In Iraq, most people do not celebrate birthdays, as no one records the day most babies are born. Instead, each city or village keeps a list of all the babies that are born each year.

Each morning of the past school year, Nadia saw Maryam watch out the window wistfully as groups of high school girls happily chatted and laughed as they walked by the Sefros' apartment window. One morning, Nadia had finally asked Maryam the question she had been wondering all along: "Why don't you introduce yourself to some of these girls? Surely they don't bite!"

Maryam had not replied. She just shrugged silently and turned away, her dark eyes looking sadder than they had before Nadia had asked her question.

Nadia's 12 year old brother Adam was also sad and lonely at the middle school, but he managed to hide it better. He kept himself very busy in the store, working long hours beside his father. As the oldest son in the family, he knew it was his duty to learn the family business.

Adam had a hard time making friends because he was so busy. In addition, many of the boys his age were already in "gangs," and many of these gangs were always in trouble with the police for violence and stealing.

Nadia was luckier than her older siblings. She had a friend from her class named Kendra, who lived right down the block. Kendra had bounced over the first day the Sefro family had moved into the neighborhood almost six months ago.

The first thing Kendra had asked Nadia was "what grade are y'all in?" When Nadia had shyly answered "fourth," Kendra had let out a whoop of joy, held up her hand and said "Me, too! High five, sister!"

Nadia was not at all sure what "high five" meant, but she somehow knew that she should also hold up her hand. She jumped as the other girl slapped her hand as hard as she could, but quickly realized through Kendra's tone of voice and smile that it was a friendly gesture.

"It must be one of those strange American habits or customs that Mama always warned us about," she thought.

Even though Nadia began fourth grade in the middle of the school year, she never had to worry about breaking into any groups or making new friends. Kendra was very popular and quickly introduced her to all of the other kids her age. The Sefro family with their dark brown skin and hair fit right in the neighborhood, which was filled with children of different races and colors who all played together happily.

The only problem for Nadia was that when the neighborhood kids were ready to play, the Sefro children were always expected to work in the family's store. They did lots of jobs, mainly sorting returnable bottles and cans, stocking shelves, sweeping floors and helping customers.

It sure didn't seem fair to Nadia that she was the only one in her class who didn't get to play in the neighborhood after school. Even the summer days were filled with work to be done.

Nadia's thoughts were interrupted as pesky five year old Daniel whined from the back seat. "When are we going to be there? I'm tired of driving."

"In a few minutes, kids," Mrs. Sefro replied. "Remember, I told you that it always takes one hour or more to get to your cousins' house."

"But you know I can't tell time," Daniel replied, still using his whiny voice.

"Quiet!" Nadia's father spoke to his youngest son with one firm word and gave Daniel one of his glares. Like most Chaldean men, Mr. Sefro never said much. He automatically expected Daniel and all of his children to behave and to respect him, and they always did.

The rest of the car trip was quiet except for the loud newscast that Mr. Sefro played from his radio station. There were only two radio stations allowed to be played in the family car: the Iraqi music station and the news station.

"Once again, the Detroit schools have published the lowest graduation rate in the state," the radio blared. "The schools are some of the worst in the nation."

Nadia knew that the Detroit schools had a terrible reputation for a long time. While there were dedicated teachers who really wanted to teach the children, many of them were discouraged about all of the problems.

Nadia also knew that there were a lot of parents who just didn't care if their kids did well in school or not, and the teachers had a very hard time getting those children to behave and learn. Nadia was glad that her parents cared about her school and helped her with her homework.

“The school buildings in Detroit are all falling apart,” the radio talk show continued. “They are in constant disrepair.”

To the Sefro family, the Detroit school buildings were not so bad. In fact, they were a big improvement over the school buildings they had to attend in Iraq. In their old country, their schools were often mud huts that had no air circulation despite the very hot temperatures.

Mr. and Mrs. Sefro were more upset about the violence in the Detroit schools than they were about the buildings. It seemed that the children spent more time worrying about their safety than they did about their studies. Almost every day on the news was a report of some student in the city who was shot or stabbed by another student. Maryam even knew one of the students that had been stabbed last year.

“The schools in these suburban towns are much better than the schools in the big city,” Nadia heard Mr. Sefro say to his wife after the newscast was over. “As soon as we are able, I would like for us to move so that we can send our children to the better schools.”

Nadia couldn’t believe what she had heard. Was her father serious? Nadia liked her elementary school, but she knew that the middle school and high school had many problems.

Many students dropped out before graduation from high school, and there were others who never even tried to learn. Many of the children who did graduate could barely read.

Since the Sefros were Chaldean, or Catholic Iraqis, Nadia knew that her parents would rather send their children to one of the Catholic schools in Detroit. However, these schools were expensive!

In addition, if they went to a Catholic school, the Sefros would have to find their own transportation since the school bus would not pick them up near their house. The family only owned one vehicle, which had to be used for the family business.

So all factors considered, they really had no choice but to attend their neighborhood schools.

"Where would we move? When would we move?" Nadia thought. Many other questions came flooding into her mind after hearing her father's comment. However, she kept her excited thoughts to herself because she knew her parents were not speaking to her, and that she should not be listening to their private conversation.

She wondered if they would move into a large castle house with a yard. She imagined exactly what it might look like. Would they live near their cousins?

What schools would they go to? What would happen to all of the friends she had made in Detroit? Her new friends had helped her to forget how much she missed her friends from

Iraq. She didn't know if she could bear the thought of moving again!

Nadia's thoughts were interrupted as the crowded car pulled up their cousins' long and winding driveway. "We're here!" her two year old sister Eppa announced happily. "Out of car seat please."

"Just a minute, wait your turn!" Mrs. Sefro laughed as her other four children piled quickly out of the car. Nadia's cousins Hanna and Fatia ran out to greet the Sefros.

"So good to see you," Fatia said as she reached down to pick up Eppa. Fatia was the same age as Maryam, and they were best friends as well as cousins.

Nadia was so glad her sister had someone her age to talk to in America. However, Fatia and Maryam lived over an hour apart and were very different.

Fatia had been born in America, and had a lot of friends. She tried to include Maryam in her circle of friends, but the distance between their houses didn't make it easy. Even Fatia couldn't seem to offer Maryam any tips on how to make her own friends in the big city.

"Come on Nadia, I want to show you our new swimming pool!" Hanna nearly shrieked as she grabbed her cousin's hand.

Even though Hanna was only a year older than Nadia, they had never met before the Sefro family moved to America. Yet it seemed as if they had known each other forever.

"A swimming pool. Oh boy!" Daniel yelled as he ran after the girls. The other kids also looked excited as they all hurried around the large and beautiful brick house and peered into the back yard.

"A HUGE swimming pool," Hanna said proudly. "What do you think?"

Nadia's mouth hung open wide as she caught sight of the beautiful blue swimming pool. She had heard stories about the pools in Iraq, but only the very rich people owned them there. She had never known any family who actually had a real pool in their yard.

"It's great," shouted Adam. "Can I jump in and try it out?"

Immediately the other kids joined in the chorus of "please can we swim? Please, please?" Nadia's heart seemed to skip a beat as she waited for her parents to reply.

"Did you bring your bathing suits?" asked Aunt Sheila, who had come out from inside as soon as she heard all the commotion.

Nadia's heart sank. She knew it was too good to be true. Of course they didn't even own bathing suits, so they would never be able to try out their cousins' pool. Life just wasn't fair!

"It's so hot out that our clothes will dry quickly," said Adam. "Can't we swim with our clothes on?"

"That is not proper," Mr. Sefro replied sternly. "And besides, it is not that hot. You don't know what hot is until..."

"You've walked through an Iraqi desert with no water," the kids finished his sentence for him. Even though Mr. Sefro was very strict about being interrupted, he put a slight smile on his face. "You should be glad we worked hard to get you to America," he continued.

Nadia winced. She was tired of hearing about the Iraqi desert. She knew all about how hard her parents had it in Iraq. She also knew how hard they had worked to save to come to America, and that they had to pay good money for their children to have English lessons while they were still in Iraq. They started these lessons when the children were very young so that they would be prepared for their new country.

Mr. Sefro finished his stern lecture with "you are lucky enough without swimming in a big fancy pool." By this time, both Uncle Mike and Aunt Sheila were rolling their eyes and laughing behind Mr. Sefro.

Nadia really liked her Uncle Mike and Aunt Sheila. Uncle Mike was her father's younger brother, but he had been in the United States for over 20 years and had done very well with his stores.

Soon after Uncle Mike had arrived in America, he had met Aunt Sheila, a feisty modern woman whose family had come from Iraq many years ago. They immediately fell in love, and were married a year after they met.

Uncle Mike was thrilled that in America he could choose his own bride. In Iraq, a matchmaker like the one who hitched up Nadia's parents arranged most of the marriages.

Aunt Sheila was so different from the Chaldean women that Nadia knew from the old country. She had always worked outside the home, she was allowed to drive a car, and she often wore pants instead of skirts. Many of her clothes were stylish and fancy.

Nadia had never owned any new clothes. Instead, she wore plain skirts and blouses which were handed down from Maryam after they no longer fit her.

Even though Nadia giggled at the faces her aunt and uncle were making behind her father's back, she fought back tears of disappointment about the swimming pool. She could see that the other kids were sad, too. Yet they knew better than to argue with their father. Chaldean fathers might not say very much, but they expected their children to follow their orders without question.

The disappointment hung heavy in the air as the kids shuffled into the house. Mrs. Sefro tried to cheer everyone up. "At least it's air conditioned in this house, so we can be very comfortable without swimming," she said.

"I have an idea," Aunt Sheila suddenly chimed in cheerfully. "Instead of being sad, each guest should look around the room for a special package with your name on it."

She smiled a big smile. "I hid the packages carefully, so you have to look hard. Don't open your package until all of them have been found."

Nadia decided to put the pool out of her mind as she joined her siblings and cousins in the search for packages. What could this surprise possibly be? It wasn't Christmas or any other holiday, but she didn't want to remind her aunt of that in case it would cause her to change her mind about the mystery gift.

One by one, the children found the brightly wrapped boxes with their names on them. Pretty soon, Nadia was the only one who had not found hers. The other kids all eagerly helped her look for her package, since they knew they couldn't open theirs until Nadia's was found.

"There it is," Daniel shrieked loudly as he pointed to the corner of the room. Nadia raced to where he was pointing. Sure enough, underneath the desk was a brightly wrapped box with her name on it.

"Can we open them now?" Baby Eppa asked as she tore open her wrapping paper.

"Sure," laughed Aunt Sheila. "Go for it."

Nadia's heart skipped a beat as she felt the package and noticed it was soft. She peered at the tag taped on the outside. "Lovingly made for Nadia by Aunt Sheila, August 2001," she read out loud.

"A new swimsuit," Adam shouted. He had opened his without analyzing the package. He proudly held up a pair of red swim trunks just his size.

Squeals of delight filled the room as each of Nadia's siblings opened his or her package. "Plus a matching towel," laughed Maryam.

"Last one in the pool is a rotten egg!" yelled Hanna.

"Me not rotten egg," yelled Eppa as she tore her clothes off.

"I never heard that American saying before," laughed Nadia.

"Well, you better hurry up before you find out how it works," said Fatia playfully. She already had her suit on and was ready to get in the water.

The Sefro boys and girls quickly divided up into the different rooms to dress into their swimsuits. Nadia was very excited. She never owned a bathing suit before, and she had certainly never gone swimming in a real swimming pool! This was going to be an exciting day.

A few minutes later all of the kids were in the pool having the time of their lives. Even though it was a large pool, every part of it was being used! The pool had a slide and a diving board, and Adam, Fatia and Hanna jumped in the deep end fearlessly.

Nadia preferred to float in an inner tube in the shallow end near baby Eppa and Daniel. Maryam sat thoughtfully on the edge of the pool and lazily dangled her feet in the water.

All of the parents sat near the deep end of the pool cheerfully catching up on the family news while watching the children. Occasionally even the adults would splash water on themselves to keep cool. Uncle Mike had a funny chef's hat on as he flipped chicken on the barbecue grill. It smelled delicious!

Nadia thought how happy she felt to be in her cousins' pool with family all around. In Iraq they were never able to cool down until the sun was long gone. Often they even had to sleep on top of their roof to be sure they caught a breeze. All of the roofs in Iraq were flat for this reason.

Nadia continued day dreaming when she suddenly realized that she was staring in the direction of her uncle and the delicious aroma of the barbecue chicken. Uncle Mike winked at her when he noticed that she was watching him. She smiled and winked back at her uncle.

Even though she missed her friends back home, Nadia was really beginning to like America.

Chapter 2
The Robbery

Nadia finished stocking the last carton of milk into the store's big cooler and looked up at the clock on the wall. She saw that it was only 7:00 pm, which meant that there was still time enough to fill the pop cooler before they closed the store.

"Hey girl, what's happening?" a familiar voice interrupted Nadia's thoughts. She turned around to see her friends Kendra and Keisha coming towards her on their in-line blades.

"Hurry and take those blades off before my dad sees them," Nadia warned.

"Girl, this floor is so old and dirty! Our blades aren't gonna matter," Kendra said. Nadia knew that her friend was teasing because Kendra did quickly go back towards the door, then she turned around and smiled.

"Just came by to say hi. We'll see y'all later, girl, don't work too hard." With that, she waved and skated away.

Nadia sighed. She was always happy to see her friends, but also embarrassed and sad that she had to work so hard while they all played. Every time they visited her, she prayed that her father would not come out and start yelling at them in his broken English for marking up the store's floor. Then she would be truly disgraced.

Nadia was proud of her parents, but she knew that they were hard to understand. She had often heard the teenage customers mimicking her father's accent.

She moved towards the back room as she thought about her family and friends. Her stomach growled as she smelled the stuffed grape leaves that her mother was cooking upstairs. Mother's special Chaldean recipe called for always using fresh peppers, Swiss chard and squash from their Uncle Mike's garden.

Uncle Mike grew beautiful and plentiful fruits and vegetables of all kinds in his garden. He shared these delicious foods with all of the family. He also sold some of the produce at his own stores.

Uncle Mike's two stores were not party stores like Nadia's family owned. They were delicatessens that served sandwiches, salads and other fresh foods to businessmen and families.

Even though Nadia's father sometimes helped work in Uncle Mike's garden, Nadia knew that he really missed having his own garden. His fruit and vegetable garden was his pride and joy in the old country, and everyone in the family worked hard to see that the special old country seeds produced beautiful crops year after year.

It was so sad for Mr. Sefro that their apartment in America had no yard for a garden. The children also missed being able to play in a yard.

"Can we close early tonight?" she suddenly heard Adam's usual question. "It's getting dark early now that September is coming. You know we don't like to stay open once it's dark."

Mr. Sefro was working on the books in the small office behind the cash register where Maryam stood. Maryam winked at her sister because they both knew what their father's answer would be.

"We can't pay the bills if the doors are closed," Mr. Sefro replied, just as Nadia knew he would. Tonight, however, he sounded more worried than usual.

"We can hardly pay the bills when the doors are open, so keep working. Pop and beer need filling and the floor needs a mop."

The children all went back to their jobs obediently. The clock turned slowly as the usual evening customers came in to stock up on their cigarettes, party supplies and lottery tickets.

"Why do we sell these things to people who should not be buying them?" Nadia had asked her father when their store first opened.

"That is a good question, Nadia," her father had replied sadly. "Unfortunately, when a man is new to a country, he takes any job he can get to support his family. Not very many smart people who have lived here long want to run a store like this in the middle of the city. For now, this store allows me to earn a good living for our family, but I always have my eye open for a better business to run."

It made Nadia sad to think that her father did not feel good about the store their family owned. She understood how he felt, but she felt that there were some good things about the store.

"Father, don't forget that many people buy their food from us," she reminded him. "That's good, isn't it?"

Mr. Sefro's response had surprised her. "I am glad to sell food to these people," he said, "but they deserve to have larger grocery stores like they have in the suburbs. There are no big grocery stores in Detroit right now, so people without cars have no choice but to pay high prices to buy their food and drink at the small local party stores like ours."

Nadia thought about what her father had said. During the day, the Sefros' store had nice people shopping there to stock up on food and drink. If they had somewhere else to go, the party store would have to be supported by the evening customers, who often smelled like beer or wine and had bloodshot eyes and slurred speech.

Many of these evening customers were mean and nasty. For example, there was the old lady who begged on the corner all day. When she finally got $2.00, she would come and buy her next half-pint of vodka.

Then there were the teenage boys who constantly tried to come in and purchase cigarettes or liquor even though it was against the law.

In Michigan a person had to be at least 18 years old to buy cigarettes and 21 years old to buy alcohol. Mr. Sefro was very strict about following the law, so he built his office right behind the register. Then Maryam could call him up whenever she had a customer who wanted to buy beer, wine, liquor or cigarettes.

When Mr. Sefro refused to sell these items to under-aged people, it often meant he lost sales for his store. However, he knew that he could get into a lot of trouble if he broke the law. More importantly, he did not believe that young people should smoke or drink.

Often, after Mr. Sefro would refuse to sell to the neighborhood teens, they would leave the store yelling “damn you Arabs” as they spit all over the front door and windows.

Nadia was glad that she didn’t have to work the cash registers and deal with these people. She filled the last section of the pop cooler and turned around again to check the time. The clock said 7:45 pm, but as Adam had noted earlier, it was getting dark sooner each night and she could barely see outside.

Mr. Sefro was nowhere in sight. She knew that now was a good time for her and Maryam to sneak a snack.

As she slowly shuffled towards her sister, she noticed two men enter the store. She didn't recognize them, but she couldn't really see their faces from where she stood.

She grabbed two bags of nuts and hurried towards her sister, who was staring at the two customers with a worried look on her face. Now what was Maryam thinking about? She wished her sister would have a happy look once in awhile.

Nadia jumped as she realized what her sister was frowning about. Both men had masks on their faces and guns pointed towards Maryam as they approached the cash register from the other direction.

"Give us all your money and no one gets hurt!" snarled one of the men, who didn't look much older than Maryam.

"We don't wanna hurt no one, we just want cash," the other man said. Nadia thought that he actually sounded a little scared.

Maryam didn't seem to be reacting. Nadia thought Maryam looked like she hadn't even heard the men.

"Maryam, give them the money so you don't get shot," Nadia pleaded with her sister. The family knew all about robberies.

They had heard of many Chaldean party storeowners who had been shot to death when they refused to give up their hard-earned money.

The meaner of the two men fired a shot in the air as he moved toward Maryam. "You better give it up now, lady," he warned fiercely. The shot startled Maryam into reality as she opened her cash register drawer and threw the money at the men.

"Get out of here!" she screamed. "I hate you. I hate Detroit. I hate America. There are only bad and mean people in America who steal all that we work for."

Nadia froze. Had Maryam lost her mind? Why would she say such things when the men had guns? Surely they would now be angry enough to shoot at her!

However, the men didn't care about the insults. They had grabbed the cash and disappeared into the dark night, leaving Maryam sobbing and Nadia running to comfort her sister.

"Why did you yell at them? They had guns, they could have killed you!" Nadia, so wise for her ten years, scolded her older sister. "You know the rule: give them the money and let them go."

By now Mr. Sefro and Adam had come out from the back room. "We heard a shot. What happened, what is going on?" her father yelled.

"Call the police, we've been robbed," Maryam screamed between sobs. "Father, I had to give them our money or they would have shot me."

Adam picked up the phone and began dialing 911. Mr. Sefro ran over to his daughters.

"My children, my children are you hurt?" he asked. He hugged Maryam tightly. "Do not worry about the money, Maryam. You are okay. That is all that matters."

Nadia had never seen her father hug anyone since they left the old country and he had to say goodbye to Grandma Sefro. Maryam broke down in her father's arms as he comforted her.

Mr. Sefro then turned to his younger daughter. "My Nadia, my Nadia, are you okay?" Mr. Sefro asked. "Please come here and let me see you." Nadia went to her father and finally let the tears come. By now even Mr. Sefro was weeping loudly as he hugged both of his daughters.

Nadia had thought that her father would be angry about the money, but he didn't seem to care at all about that. He seemed to be much more concerned about his daughters.

"Adam, lock the doors up now," he ordered his oldest son. "From now on, we close each night at 7:00. I don't care about any money. I care about my children. Thank goodness you are all safe."

Just then the police cars rode up with sirens blaring. Two policemen jumped out.

"Which way did they go?" they asked as they looked up and down the street. Mr. Sefro looked at Maryam and Nadia for a reply, and Nadia pointed to the left. One of the policemen ran off in that direction while the other officer came in with his notepad.

"We need to ask you a lot of questions about these men so we can find them and put them in jail," the police officer with the notepad explained gently to Nadia and Maryam.

At that moment, Mrs. Sefro, who had heard the commotion, walked in with Daniel and Eppa.

"What in the world is going on?" she cried. She didn't wait for an answer as she rushed over towards her children. Nadia could see in her mother's eyes that she knew what had happened.

Maryam rushed to see her mother. "Mother, today's money is all gone. How will we possibly pay our bills?" she cried. "I couldn't help it. I had to give them the money or they were going to shoot me."

"As long as everyone is safe, that's all that matters," Mrs. Sefro assured her children.

Nadia could tell that her mother was upset but was trying to be calm. "Let's finish with the policeman and all go upstairs and have a nice dinner," Mrs. Sefro suggested softly.

The first policeman had returned to the store after having no luck finding the robbers. A neighbor had seen the men run away on foot, and pointed out to the police where one of them had dropped a mask.

"I'm bringing the tracking dog back out to try to run them down, using this mask as a clue," the policeman told them as he left.

For the next hour Nadia and Maryam told the second policeman everything that had happened and tried to give complete descriptions of both men.

The policeman told Maryam that she did the right thing by giving the men the money. He also gave the Sefro family some kind words of advice.

"Never leave your girl alone at the register, and you should buy a security system so we can get here more quickly next time," he said. "Most importantly, you should install bulletproof glass like all of the other stores around here have. It could save one of your lives."

Nadia felt a twinge of pain as she saw the look on her father's face. Her Uncle Mike had told father to put in bulletproof glass, but Mr. Sefro liked to deal with his customers face to face, with no glass between them.

“I like to see the people who are my customers,” he had said when they first opened the store. “I like them to know that I trust them. Bulletproof glass is too impersonal for me.”

About the time the questioning was finished, the other police officer had returned to the store with his dog. Both the officer and the dog looked very discouraged.

“We lost their scent about three blocks up, and we are out of all other clues,” he announced grimly. “These two will be tough to find.”

After the policemen left, the Sefro family walked together to their tiny apartment in silence. As they climbed up the stairs, Nadia wondered where in the world they would find the money for a new security system, especially if they were going to lock the doors earlier each night as it got darker. She could tell that her father was thinking the same thing.

“Come children, we all need some dinner and rest, and then things won’t seem so terrible,” Mr. Sefro told them.

Although Nadia was not hungry, she dutifully joined her family at the dinner table. As she looked around, she noticed that her mother and Maryam both had red and puffy eyes. Her father still had a very worried look on his face. Her two brothers and baby sister didn’t seem to even know that anything had happened as they hungrily waited for their food.

“Before we eat tonight, we will say a special prayer to our God,” Mr. Sefro said. “Please everyone, bow your heads and show respect.”

Nadia obediently followed her father's request and bowed her head. She noticed that everyone else, even baby Eppa, did the same.

"Dear Father, we thank you that our beloved family is safe and together," Mr. Sefro began. "We also bless those family members that we had to leave behind in Iraq. We pray for their safety and happiness."

He paused, and then continued. "We especially pray for the terrible men who robbed us tonight and pointed guns at my Maryam."

Nadia was surprised to hear her father pray for these men, and was also surprised to hear his voice break as if he were going to cry again.

Mr. Sefro stopped the prayer for a moment and Nadia could see that he had tears in his eyes. He took a deep breath and continued.

"God, we ask you to help us pay our bills this month, and we ask you to help the business in our store to improve so we can always pay our bills."

It seemed as if the prayer was done, but Mr. Sefro's tone was so serious that none of the children dared to look up. There was a long and drawn out silence before Mrs. Sefro finally spoke to help her husband finish the blessing.

"Through Jesus Christ our Lord. Bless this food we eat. Amen," she said.

"AMEN," the children repeated after her in relief. Adam, Daniel and Eppa immediately started eating their stuffed grape leaves quickly. "Good dinner, mom," Adam said in between mouthfuls.

Maryam, Nadia, and their parents all sat at the table, silently picking at their food. Nadia knew Maryam was wondering the same thing she was wondering: how serious was the money situation? She knew better than to ask, but was it possible that they would have to sell the store and apartment and return to Iraq? She was really starting to feel at home in America.

The more Nadia tried to push thoughts of moving back to Iraq out of her mind, the more she remembered about her home country. The unbearable heat in Iraq had been bad enough for healthy people, but the real heartbreak for the family had come with the death of the tiny baby that Mama had between Eppa and Daniel.

The baby's name had been David, and he had been small and sickly since the day he was born. Mama had a hard time feeding him as he often refused her breast milk, which was spoiled from the record breaking heat that year.

Finally came the terrible day when the baby died because he could not be properly nourished. The baby's death was devastating to the Sefro family, and they could not bear to talk about him. Nadia pictured his sweet face as she played aimlessly with her food.

Despite the baby's death, the Sefros had stayed in Iraq until the "straw that broke the camel's back" as the Americans would say. The final factor causing them to move to America was when the family store was destroyed and looted by people who worked for Saddam Hussein, the cruel leader of Iraq. Saddam and his workers had tortured and killed many people, and the constant fighting in the country finally became more than the family could take.

The sad memories filled Nadia's mind until she could not help herself anymore. Again, the tears came pouring down her cheeks.

"Maryam and Nadia, you may be excused," Mr. Sefro said gently. Nadia looked up to see that Maryam was also crying and had not touched her food.

Nadia gratefully jumped up and headed for her bedroom. Maryam was getting out of her chair, too, only she moved much slower than her younger sister did. She also picked up her and Nadia's plates and brought them over to the sink.

After she put down the plates, Maryam suddenly surprised the rest of the family by going around the table, hugging each person tightly.

“From now on, I promise I will be nicer to each of you.” she said over and over through her tears. “I love you all and have been acting terribly.”

Nadia joined her sister in hugging each of her family members. All of her family members returned her hugs, and soon Nadia felt much better.

“No matter what else happens, we still have a happy family,” she thought as she headed for her room.

Chapter 3
Mother's New Job

"I'll be back in time for you to help close the store down," Nadia's mom said as she put on her makeup. "Check the dinner every few minutes and get Eppa up about 4:00. Please make sure both kids have a healthy snack."

"Good luck, mom. I know you'll do well at the job interview," Nadia said. "I'll take care of everything here."

Mrs. Sefro looked very pretty today. She had her dark hair up in a fancy bun, and was all dressed up in her red silky dress, which was the only nice dress that she owned.

Nadia noticed that her mother also looked nervous. She had never had a job interview before. In fact, she had never worked outside the family businesses.

In Iraq, the man was the boss of the household. Most men, including Mr. Sefro, would not allow their wives to leave the family and work for someone else. However, Nadia knew that her father had changed his mind since the family financial situation was not good. The extra money her mother earned would help pay the bills and save the family business and apartment.

It also helped that Aunt Sheila and Uncle Mike had convinced Nadia's parents that having Mrs. Sefro work for the casino was the American thing to do. Most women in America worked outside the house.

“There’s no reason to be nervous, Mom,” Nadia assured her. “You know that they need good workers like you at the new casino. You learned all about dealing cards, and Aunt Sheila told you that you will be speaking with a very nice man.”

Even though Nadia sounded hopeful, deep inside she was worried that her mother might not get the casino job due to her heavy accent.

Evidently Mrs. Sefro did not pick up on her daughter’s concern. She turned around to smile at Nadia.

“You’re right, sweetie, thank you,” she said as she kissed her daughter. “You have been a big help.”

Nadia was actually glad to have a few hours away from the store. She never had responsibility for both Daniel and Eppa before, but surely it was easier than stocking shelves of food. Besides, Maryam, Dad and Adam were right downstairs if she needed them.

“Bye sweetie,” Mrs. Sefro called as she closed and locked the door behind her.

Nadia peeked in on Eppa, who was still napping, and then went to talk to Daniel.

“Please sit quietly and watch television for awhile so I can do my homework,” she told her little brother.

“Okay,” said Daniel sweetly. He was watching an American cartoon on television and seemed very content not to move.

Nadia took out her schoolbooks and carefully selected the largest one, the math book. She liked to do her math first because it was easier for her. The other subjects were more difficult since she was not as good as her classmates at speaking and reading the English language.

As she opened the book and started figuring out the math problems, the doorbell rang.

“Who could that be?” she wondered out loud. It couldn’t be a stranger because a stranger wouldn’t be able to get through dad’s office to go up the stairs.

“Hey girl, it’s me, Kendra,” she heard the familiar voice through the door. “Your sister told me you’re not working in the store tonight, so I thought maybe you could come out and play for once.”

Nadia sighed. Just once she would like to play with her friends after school. They always had so much fun during recess, but she felt like she was missing a lot more fun when the rest of them played together after school.

She carefully unlocked the extra strong lock Mr. Sefro had put on the door after the robbery. Her friend stood there with a big grin on her face.

“Well, aren’t you gonna invite me in?” she asked. “I’ve never been inside your place before.”

Nadia hesitated. Her mother didn't say anything about having a friend in the house, and she knew that she should be concentrating on watching Eppa and Daniel and doing her homework.

"You can come in for a minute, but I'm watching my brother and sister while my mother goes to a job interview," she told Kendra.

"Girl, they never let you have any fun," teased her friend. She looked around at the small apartment.

"Hey, y'all got a nice place here," she said politely. "Where is your mama going to work?"

"I hope at the new casino," replied Nadia. "My Aunt Sheila has a job there dealing cards. She told my mother they needed a lot more help. We need the money! Since the robbery, we had to put a new security system into our family business, and that was expensive."

"If your mom goes to work, who is gonna take care of your house and the little ones?" asked Kendra.

"Somebody in the family," Nadia shrugged. "Maybe me. Maybe Maryam or Adam. Or maybe all of us will take turns. I don't know what Mama's work hours are going to be."

"Girl, you never get a break, do you?" Kendra asked again.

"I get lots of breaks," Nadia replied defensively, "but when you have a family business, everyone in the family has to help."

"I guess so," Kendra said. "It's just that you miss a lot of fun when you work every day."

"I don't care," Nadia shrugged again.

Deep inside she knew she did care. She would much rather be skating with Kendra than sorting nasty returnable pop and beer bottles at the store, or filling coolers. However, she knew she had no choice.

"Maybe if my mom gets a job, I will have to watch Eppa and Daniel, and I won't have to work at the store," she said hopefully. "Then I'll be able to hang out more."

"Yeah, that'll be lots of fun hanging around with your pesky little brother and sister," teased Kendra. "Well, I'll be going now. I need to go see what the gang's up to this afternoon."

Nadia watched Kendra skip out the door. She really wished she were free to join her friend. If she had time to hang out all they time, maybe she'd be as popular as Kendra.

Her thoughts were interrupted by her father's booming voice. "I see everything's going fine up here," he said, winking at her. "This is a lot easier than sweeping floors downstairs, isn't it?"

"Yes," Nadia replied. "Father, if Mama gets this job, am I going to watch the younger children each day? If so, who will take my place working at the store?"

"Nadia, that is not for you to worry about," her father replied firmly. "We don't even know if she is going to be hired for the job. If she is hired, we have no idea what her hours will be. You just be willing to help wherever we ask you to help."

"Of course, father," Nadia answered. "I think I hear Eppa, so I better go check on her."

"You do that," her father said. "I'll be back downstairs if you need me."

The rest of the afternoon flew by as Nadia rushed between Eppa, Daniel, checking dinner and trying to squeeze in some math problems. She was very surprised when she heard the key in the door and saw her mother walk in the room.

"Mother, why are you back so soon?" she asked.

"Honey, it's 6:00," Mrs. Sefro replied. "I've been gone for hours."

"How did it go?" Nadia asked. She couldn't really tell if her mother was happy.

"They hired me!" Mrs. Sefro exclaimed. "I start working the second shift next week. This job pays very well and should be the answer to all of our money problems."

"Congratulations," Nadia said as she hugged her mother. "I knew you would do well. But who will take care of everything while you work?"

"Come now, your father already told me that you asked him that question earlier," Mrs. Sefro teased. "Didn't he tell you not to worry about it?"

She paused. "Did you feel comfortable about taking over my duties today?" she asked Nadia. "It seems you did a fine job keeping everything in order."

"Yes, time went really fast," Nadia replied. "And I like staying home and watching Daniel and Eppa more than I like working downstairs in the store."

"Well, you are a big help at the store, but you would be a bigger help here," Mrs. Sefro said. "We really need Maryam to work the cash register, and we need Adam's muscles with all the heavy stock."

"Then who would take my place at the store?" Nadia asked.

"The store can't afford another employee," Mrs. Sefro replied. "Everyone will need to work even harder to do their jobs and your job, too. They will probably all have to work later each evening to finish up the work."

“What time will you be home each night, mother?” Nadia asked.

“Not until after you are all in bed,” her mother replied. “I will work five nights per week from 3:00 until 11:00. I have to leave by 2:00 to take the bus so I arrive at work on time, so I won’t be home until after midnight.”

“But that will mean no more family dinners,” Nadia said sadly. “When are we going to see you?”

Her excitement over her mother’s job had suddenly turned to worry and sadness as she realized how long she would be away each day.

“I will see you each morning and on each of my days off,” Mrs. Sefro said. “Come now, Nadia, you are so busy all the time, I hardly see you even when I am not working.”

Nadia knew that her mother was right, but still a sad and sinking feeling had come over her.

“Cheer up, honey,” Mrs. Sefro continued to try to persuade Nadia. “This is a night to celebrate. It is good that I will be working and our family will no longer have to worry about the money.

“In fact, why don’t you go downstairs and help them close the store? Then we can have an extra special family dinner tonight. Have father bring up a special dessert.”

“Okay,” Nadia hugged her mother. “I really am happy for you and your new job.”

“Thank you, honey; I am happy about it too.” Even though Mrs. Sefro smiled as she hugged her daughter, Nadia realized that she had seen tears in her mother’s eyes.

Was it possible that despite how her mother was acting, she was sad about working? Maybe she had no choice, and had mixed feelings about the job like Nadia did. It was good that the family would be earning more money, but it was not good that mother would be gone so much of the time.

Nadia’s spirits lifted when she saw her father’s face. Mr. Sefro looked more happy and relaxed than he had looked since the robbery.

“Sure, we’ll celebrate tonight,” he said after Nadia told him about the special dessert. “You go pick something out and bring it up to your mother. Come back down and help us close the store. We will lock the doors a little early tonight so we can all have a good time together.”

Mr. Sefro must have noticed that Nadia was a bit sad.

“It is a good thing, Nadia that we can provide for our family,” he told his daughter. “If mother does not work, we can’t make enough money to keep the store open. That would mean that we may have to go back to Iraq, and I know you don’t want that.”

"I would like to go back," Maryam suddenly piped in her opinion from behind the cash register. "I miss my friends and the rest of our family. America is no better than Iraq."

Nadia was surprised at her sister's outburst, and was sure that her father would be angry with Maryam for what she had said.

Instead, Mr. Sefro sighed. "Maryam, my dear, one day you will join the rest of us and open your eyes to all that America has to offer us," he said. "I miss my friends and family, too, but we would like to think that we are here to stay and it is time for you to accept that. Now please act happy tonight for the sake of your mother."

Nadia could see tears forming in Maryam's eyes. She prayed for her sister to keep her composure in front of their father. If she started crying and continued talking about how unhappy she was, it would ruin the family celebration.

Luckily, Mr. Sefro pretended he didn't see Maryam's tears.

"Hurry and finish up, girls, we have a big night," he said. "Maryam, you lock the door while I find Adam and take a look through the store for final customers before we clear the cash register."

The next hour was spent in busy silence as the Sefro family closed their store down for the evening. Nadia could not stop thinking about mother's new job and how it would change the family. However, she knew her father was right: they should all act happy for the sake of their mother. Mama was the one who would have to work away from home and miss her family the most.

"The rest of us will still be together most of the time," she thought to herself, "and that is a very good thing."

Chapter 4
Twin Towers

"Boys and girls, we have an important announcement about a serious tragedy that is occurring in our country as we speak." The principal's voice bellowed over the PA system. "Children, please. I need everyone's immediate and complete attention."

The tone of Mr. Johnson's voice alarmed Nadia, and she could tell that her fifth grade classmates were also concerned. The usual commotion in the room stopped suddenly. In fact, it became so quiet that Nadia was afraid that everyone could hear her stomach growling.

It seemed like a long time before the principal finally continued his message. "There is a national emergency, but there is no reason for any of you to be afraid as long as we all remain calm and follow certain safety precautions."

Nadia's heart began racing. She was familiar with national emergencies. They were common in Iraq, where she used to live. But what serious tragedy could possibly happen in America?

As if he were reading her thoughts, Mr. Johnson continued. "There have been some terrible plane crashes in New York City, Washington D.C. and Pennsylvania. It appears that these plane crashes were planned by somebody who is angry at America.

He continued. "We do not know who planned these crashes, but to protect ourselves we are locking the entire school for the rest of the day. We will not be going outside for recess. Please report any unusual visitors to the office immediately."

He concluded," we will keep you posted as soon as we hear more information. Once again, children, there is no need for alarm."

The dead silence in the room following the announcement was quickly replaced by an anxious chatter of children's voices. Above the chatter were a few stifled sobs.

Loudest of all the cries came from James Jones. "My dad is in New York City," he cried. "He is flying back today. What if he was killed in one of the plane crashes?"

"Now James, there is no need to jump to any conclusions," replied Mrs. Patterson, Nadia's teacher. "There are many people and planes in New York City. You shouldn't worry about anything until we hear more information."

As usual, Mrs. Patterson's gentle voice was soothing to her students. However, Nadia couldn't help notice that her young teacher was twitching nervously, and seemed unsure what to say to the children as the buzz in the room gradually grew louder.

Nadia decided to help her teacher out. She raised her hand and started talking before her teacher acknowledged her.

"Mrs. Patterson," she said. "Back in Iraq, when we were in class and there was a national emergency, we would sing songs."

Her teacher smiled at Nadia, who was one of her most energetic and upbeat students.

"Class, I think that Nadia has a great idea," said Mrs. Patterson. "If we all sing some songs together, it might make us feel better. What songs shall we sing?"

"How about some Motown music?" Tommy Franklin suggested. The class giggled at his idea. Tommy always reminded them that he was a distant relative of Aretha Franklin, the famous Motown singer from Detroit.

One of the first things Nadia had learned about Detroit was from Tommy. He had informed her that "Motown" was short for "Motor Town." Detroit is often called the "Motor Town" or "Motor City" since many of the big automobile factories are in the Detroit area. "Motown Music" is a style of music that originated in Detroit.

Nadia piped up again before her teacher could reply to Tommy's suggestion. "How about if we sang a song about America?" she asked.

"How about 'God Bless America?'" Kendra jumped into the conversation. Kendra's father was a preacher and they often sang religious songs at their house.

Mrs. Patterson replied quickly. “Sorry children, we are not allowed to sing religious songs in our schools,” she said. “Remember when we studied the separation of religion and government?”

She stopped. “I have another idea. How about singing our national anthem? Does anybody want to start us out?” She looked around hopefully, but nobody volunteered.

“Does anybody besides me KNOW the national anthem?” Mrs. Patterson asked, sounding perturbed. The students in the class looked at each other quizzically.

John Adamson raised his hand. “That’s what we sing before baseball and football games, right?” he asked.

“Yes, John,” the teacher replied. “Do you know the words?”

John shrugged his shoulders. “Not really,” he mumbled.

“Class, I am shocked that none of you know the words to the most important song in our country,” Mrs. Patterson said. “We are changing our lesson plan for today. Everyone please get out a piece of paper and begin copying down the words to our national anthem.”

Several groans came out from the class. “What happened to the singing?” asked Kendra.

“We will sing soon enough,” replied Mrs. Patterson. “First we need an important social studies lesson.”

The rest of the morning was depressingly eerie. Mrs. Patterson wrote the words to the national anthem on the blackboard between lectures about how proud they should all be to live in America. The children dutifully copied the words to the song onto their papers. There was no sign of the snickering and whispering that usually went on during these types of assignments.

Right before lunchtime, the principal came over the PA again. His voice sounded drained but calmer than it had earlier that morning.

“Children, all the other airplanes in the country have safely landed,” he announced. “All of you can feel safe in our school building. However, as a precaution, we will still have indoor recess today.”

Mr. Johnson paused. “A lot of terrible things have happened to our country this morning, and we suggest you speak to your parents in more detail about these events when you get home this afternoon.”

The hush in the room after the principal signed off continued through lunchtime. When they returned from lunch, Nadia noticed that Mrs. Patterson looked like she had been crying. The kids all shared her gloomy attitude, and it seemed like one of the longest afternoons of Nadia's life.

She couldn't wait until the final bell rang. She usually walked home with Kendra, but today she didn't even bother waiting for her best friend.

Instead Nadia ran the whole way home, anxious to see her parents. Not only did she want to be sure they were safe, she had to find out what they had to say about the situation. She was glad that Tuesday was her mother's day off.

Mrs. Sefro greeted Nadia anxiously. The television was on in the background, which was very unusual.

"Let's sit and talk while you have a snack," she said. She put a piece of melon at Nadia's plate and motioned her to sit down.

"Nadia, these airplanes intentionally crashed into buildings and killed thousands of people," Mrs. Sefro informed her. "President Bush feels that this was an act of war."

Nadia's heart raced. "Are we going to have wars all around us in the United States, like we did in Iraq?" she asked anxiously. "What I mean is, will there be bomb threats all the time, and people killed in the streets?"

"I sure hope not, but I don't know," Mrs. Sefro sighed. "The best we can do is all wait for answers. Right now, they are still trying to save people from the buildings which are burning."

Both Nadia and her mother had their attention diverted back to the television set, where the words "SPECIAL REPORT" were flashing in big letters across the screen.
What Nadia saw on the screen shocked her. There was a picture of a building, which looked very tall. As she sat there watching, one airplane flew right into the building. Instantly a fire started.

Immediately after that horrible picture, there was film of a second airplane, which came from the other direction. "Crash!" This airplane flew into a tall building which adjoined the first burning building. Both the towers were now engulfed in flames.

"That looks like the Renaissance Center in downtown Detroit!" Nadia gasped. "Mother, is this happening right now in our city?"

"No dear, that happened earlier today in New York City," her mother reassured her. "This is a film of the Twin Towers. They are much taller than any building in Detroit."

For some reason, that did not calm Nadia. A million questions filled her head after witnessing these plane crashes.

"Who crashed those planes?" she asked. "Did all of the people die?"

"Nadia, many people were killed by the evil people that did this," Mrs. Sefro began to sob softly.

She put her arm around Nadia and moved closer. She didn't seem to know what to say to her daughter.

"Let's watch for a few minutes before Eppa and Daniel get up. Maybe we can learn more about what is happening."

Together they watched television scenes which reminded Nadia of the nightmares from her home country. There were film clips of dead people and injured people, followed by interviews of politicians and officials talking about who could have possibly attacked America.

Nadia thought to herself that the only good part of the film was when they showed brave firefighters rescuing people. However, many of these firefighters were still lost in the burning building and were also feared dead.

The news kept saying that many people could not be saved. They interviewed a lot of people who thought they had lost loved ones in the building, but still were not sure due to the piles of burning rubble that were on top of all of the people.

Nadia and her mother were startled when Daniel suddenly stumbled into the room, still sleepy from his nap. Mrs. Sefro snapped off the television set.

"These children are too young for this," she said. "Anyway, Nadia, it's time for you to get to work downstairs. I'm sure they need you today."

"Okay," Nadia replied reluctantly. She did not feel like going to work. She wanted to sit here and watch television and get some answers to her many questions.
She brightened up as a thought crossed her mind. "Maybe Maryam and Adam can explain some of this to me," she thought to herself as she ran out the door.

Nadia walked in the store and saw her sister showing her new friends Jane and Karen how the store's new security system worked. Nadia's father had installed cameras to record everything that went on in the store. The security system also had buttons which the cashier could push in case of another holdup. The system would alert the police immediately.

Mr. Sefro had also put bulletproof glass in front of both cash registers. Neither the family nor the customers liked the glass, but since the Sefros felt that they had no choice, they were all getting used to it.

"Hey Nadia," Maryam acknowledged her sister from behind the glass. "What do you think about all this crazy stuff going on today?"

Nadia was still quite upset from the images on the television. "I don't understand who did this, do you?" she replied to her sister with a question.

Nadia's friend Karen turned her attention towards the two sisters. "What do you mean, who did this?" she asked. "Everyone knows that those stupid Arabs and Muslims from Iraq are back at it again. Those people are trained to murder innocent people!"

There was stone silence in the store. Nadia was shocked at what Karen said, and she could see that Maryam was too.

"Did you know that Iraq is where we come from?" Maryam asked quietly. Her face was flushed and she had tears in her eyes.

"No way! Girl I had no idea!" Karen replied. "You guys are Iraqis? I thought you said you were Chaldean!"

"Chaldeans are Catholic Iraqis," Nadia explained. "That was mean for you to say that Iraqis like to shoot and kill other people. It is not the truth at all." Nadia was surprised at how brave she was being, but Karen had made her angry.

"Furthermore," Nadia continued, "even though we are not Muslims, I know for a fact that the Islamic religion does not teach people to murder."

Maryam spoke up in a shaky voice to help Nadia explain. "The Muslims believe in one God with Muhammad as his prophet," she explained. "Their teachings are written in a holy book called the Koran, and they believe in prayer five times a day, fasting and sharing with the poor."

"Don't even try to convince me that Muslims, Arabs or Iraqis are any good." Karen retorted. "You are all the same: violent and evil." She turned around and stormed out the door.

No one knew what to say next. Maryam looked like she was going to burst into tears. Finally Jane broke the eerie silence that had taken over the cash register area.

"Karen is angry because her brother was killed by Iraqi soldiers," she said quietly. "He went over there a few years ago and never came back."

Nadia was stunned and could see that Maryam was, too.

"That is sad, but she can't blame us for that," Maryam said. "We were afraid of the soldiers, too. That's part of the reason we came to America."

"Karen was very close to her brother, and she will never get over his death," Jane replied. "I'm sure she didn't mean anything personal."

"Well, she sure fooled me," Nadia said. "Cheer up, Maryam. You don't need friends like that, anyway."

Suddenly they noticed that Mr. Sefro was standing there. "What's wrong, girls?" he asked.

"Karen just told us that all Iraqis do is shoot and kill people," Nadia replied quickly. "That isn't right, is it, father?"

"Her brother was killed by an Iraqi soldier," Jane explained quickly. "She's still very upset about that."

"But it's not our fault, is it father?" Maryam asked.

Mr. Sefro had a very sad look on his face. "No, of course it isn't right," he replied. "We do not support Saddam Hussein or his soldiers. That is one of the reasons we left Iraq. However, he was our leader and we were his people. Many Americans can't forget that."

"Father, Karen was one of my only friends, and now we can never be friends again," Maryam blurted out. "She decided that she doesn't like me because of where I come from, and I don't like her anymore because of what she said about my people."

"This is too complicated to talk about right now," Mr. Sefro replied. "There is work to be done."

With all the serious discussion, no one had noticed that two customers had come up to the register and were waiting to be serviced.

"Can't blame the girl for being mad at all of you," one of the customers said. He was a short fair skinned elderly man. "You are all trained to be violent against Americans, and you come into our country so you can take all of our good jobs."

Now it was Mr. Sefro's turn to get angry. "You do not know anything about our people," he said. "You can't blame a whole country for one man's actions."

He pointed to the door. "Please leave. We don't need customers like you."

Nadia was shocked. She had never heard her father talk like that to a customer before. She watched as the old man left his beer bottle on the cash register and stomped out the door. Right before the door shut, he turned around and spat in Mr. Sefro's direction.

Nadia felt her face flush with anger and she could see her father was angry too. However, as he saw Nadia looking at him, he shrugged.

"Not much you can do with people like that," he said as if he didn't care about the insults. "We don't need them."

"From what I hear, you need all the customers you can get," the second customer now joined in the conversation. She was a pretty black lady about the same age as Mrs. Sefro.

"I agree with you that it's not fair for them to blame you for the wars, but people think like that all the time," she continued. "There are a lot of people who think all black people are bad. It's not worth it to get angry. It won't change anything."

"How are we supposed to feel?" asked Maryam.

"The best thing you can do is hold your head high and prove to people that they are wrong about you," the lady replied. "If you get angry and try to fight back, it just makes them even angrier. Irrational anger never solves anything."

"She is right," Mr. Sefro said. "You are a very smart lady," he said to the customer.

Then he turned to his oldest daughter. “Maryam, please ring this lady up.”

“Yes, father,” Maryam said. Nadia began helping her sister by bagging up the groceries after Maryam rang them up on the cash register.

“May I pay with a local check?” the lady asked when Maryam was finished ringing up her order.

“Certainly, ma’am, as long as you have identification,” Maryam replied politely. The lady took out her wallet and carefully pulled out her driver’s license for Maryam to examine while she wrote the check.

Maryam picked the identification up to look at it and then gasped. “Lena Boyd,” she said. “Are you the Judge Lena Boyd who I read about in the newspapers?”

“That’s me,” the kind lady smiled. “I hope you have read good things about me.”

“I have read all about how you are one of the best and most fair judges in the state,” Jane chimed in. “In fact, we talked about you in our political science class the other day.”

Judge Boyd smiled. She seemed flattered. “Thank you for the compliment,” she said. She picked up her purse and began rolling her cart outside.

“I have to go now,” she said, “but please remember what I said about how important it is to hold your heads high and prove them all wrong.”

Jane, Nadia and Maryam watched Judge Boyd walk away. They had heard what the good lady said, but at this time they had no idea how much they would have to remember the wise judge’s advice during the next several weeks.

Chapter 5
Trouble at School

Nadia walked into her classroom, not sure what to expect on the day after the tragedy in New York. She did know that President Bush believed that Middle Eastern terrorists were responsible for the plane crashes. Her parents had explained to her that many of these Arabs had lived in America and even in Detroit, and that they seemed like normal, every day people.

Nadia also had read that these terrorists were led by a man named Osama bin Laden, who was hiding out in a country called Afghanistan. Bin Laden had threatened the United States many times before. He used his Islamic religion to back up his threats, even though that religion does not teach violence.

"There are millions of peace-loving Muslims in the world," Mrs. Sefro had reassured her older children what they already knew.

Nadia's parents also told her that some of the kids in the class might associate her and other Chaldeans with these bad people from Saudi Arabia and Afghanistan. This was because Saddam Hussein had threatened the United States many times in the past.

Also, Iraq is in the same region as Afghanistan and Saudi Arabia. All of the people who come from that region have similar dark hair and skin, regardless of which country they come from.

"Most Americans can not tell the difference between a Saudi Arabian and a Chaldean," Mr. Sefro had remarked.

Nadia was relieved when Mrs. Patterson walked in the door and patted her gently on the shoulder as she walked by. She looked tired.

"Good morning, Nadia," she said. "Are you ready for a good day?" Nadia nodded in response.

A few minutes later, two more students arrived. Nadia was glad to see her friends Janet and Carol. However, instead of greeting her and sitting next to Nadia, they took seats far away from her and began to whisper to each other. Nadia felt her face flush.

"Oh well, maybe they don't see me," she thought, though she knew they probably had. She tried to concentrate on one of the news stories that her teacher had passed around for the students to read.

The more Nadia read about the tragedy in New York, the more shocked and surprised she was. It seems there were many men who had plotted for many years to kill all of those people. These terrorists had taken over control of the airplanes, threatening the pilots and passengers with knives.

These men believed that the United States was evil and powerful, and that Americans had hurt their religion and their countries in the past. They were so angry at the United

States that they were willing to die in the plane crashes along with all of the passengers who died with them.

"All the newscasters are saying that there's a bunch of you Muslim spies living all over the place that are in on this bombing." Jack Davies' voice suddenly came from the seat behind her. "Is that why your family moved here, to spy on Americans?"

Nadia turned to face Jack. "Are you talking to me?" she asked, her voice quivering.

Jack snickered rudely. Nadia was so shocked she could not think of a response. She turned back to her reading.

Her mind grew numb as she continued reading the stories. The mayor of New York had estimated it would take weeks to dig up all of the bodies, but many people still hoped that there would be some humans found alive underneath all of the rubble from the building. In the meantime, the president was planning what the United States military would do to retaliate against whoever committed this horrible act of war.

This was all like a very bad dream to Nadia. She really thought that her family would be away from the wars when they moved to America. She should have known that the United States seemed too good to be true!

She turned her attention back to the classroom, which by now was mostly full. "Why were all of the seats around me still empty?" she wondered as she looked around the room.

She waved to Kendra who was on the other side of the room. “Come sit over here, girl,” she called out to her best friend.

Kendra turned her head away, pretending not to see Nadia. Nadia again felt her face flush.

What was going on? Her parents had warned her that some people might be prejudiced against her, but she never imagined her best friends would believe that nonsense and turn their backs on her!

“Class, it’s time to get to work,” Mrs. Patterson finally spoke; obviously unaware of what was happening among her students. “This morning we will begin with Math. Please take out your books.”

Nadia didn’t know how she made it through the morning, but she did. She decided to go home for lunch rather than endure the humiliation of the lunchroom. She ran the entire way, eager to be reassured by her parents.

She burst into the store. As usual, the first person she saw was Mr. Sefro. “Father, you would not believe how terrible school was today!” she began.

“Yes, I would,” Adam’s voice interrupted Nadia. She was surprised to hear her brother. He never came home for lunch. She turned around to ask him what was going on, and was shocked at how he looked.

“Adam, what in the world happened to you? she cried out. “You look like you were in a train wreck.” He had a black eye and his entire face was swollen. He also looked like he had been crying. Nadia couldn’t remember the last time she saw him cry.

“I was suspended from school for being in a fight,” Adam said. “A bunch of those kids from the Bang Gang were calling our family bad names and threatening me. I could not take it anymore, so I hit Karl Smith, the leader of the gang. His buddies came to his rescue, but since I have no friends, it was an unfair fight.” His voice was bitter.

Mr. Sefro spoke up. “Your brother acted foolishly with his heart and not his head,” he said firmly. “Now his chance at education is in jeopardy.” He glared at his son.

“Father, they said that our family came to this country to kill more Americans,” Adam said. “They all stood in a circle and yelled insults at me. They also threatened the family, and the Bang Gang is known for violence. What could I have done?”

“You rise above it and walk away, that’s what you do,” Mr. Sefro said. He glared at Adam as if he could not his son anymore.

“Get to work since you can not go to school,” he ordered, then turned to his daughter. “Nadia, what are you doing here?” he asked.

Nadia had almost forgotten about her own troubles at school. “Father, the kids in the class were very mean to me, also," she replied. "No one would sit near me or talk to me, and I didn't want to be alone at lunch time."

For a long minute, Mr. Sefro did not seem to know what to say. He finally spoke.

"Nadia, when we moved to a new country, we knew it would be tough," he said. "We had no idea what God had in store for us. But we are a tough family and we are going to get through this together."

He paused. "Don't you remember what Judge Boyd told you yesterday about prejudice?"

"Yes, I do," Nadia replied. "But it is so hard! All of these people are so wrong about us, and I don't know what to say or do to convince them of that. I can understand why Adam felt that he had to get into a fight."

"Fighting proves nothing!" Mr. Sefro retorted. "Our religion teaches us that the only option is to do our best and leave it to Jesus to help us out. God is in charge, yet sometimes we try too hard to change things that can not be changed."

Nadia listened respectfully to her father because she knew better than to argue. However, she did not understand why God would allow all of these bad things to happen to her world.

"You better hurry and get some lunch so you don't miss any of your afternoon studies," Mr. Sefro said sternly.

Then his voice suddenly softened. "Would you like one of the hot dogs we are selling now? It's all ready to go."

He winked at his daughter. He knew that his children loved hot dogs and other American junk food, but they usually were not allowed to eat this unhealthy fare. The Chaldean diet their family normally ate was full of fruits, vegetables and other healthy foods. Mama usually took hours to prepare it all just right.

"Thank you father, a hot dog sounds perfect," Nadia said, her spirits lifting slowly. "You are right; I better hurry and eat so I can return to school."

She devoured the hot dog and ran quickly back to her classroom. She managed to get through the afternoon despite the fact that all of her friends continued to ignore her.

She followed her father's advice, and tried to rise above it.
However, by the time school was over, she was feeling pretty sad and lonely. She ran as fast as she could to her safe and loving home.

Chapter 6
Burning Dreams

Nadia awoke from her dream in a sweat. She had been dreaming that a large group of people was down in the street, chanting something like "Nadia is a spy, shoot her in the eye."

She shook her head to force herself to wake up so she could forget the dream.

It certainly was believable that her classmates would do something like this to her. However, as usual, a big part of her dream was confusing.

The group of chanters in her dreams included not only her classmates but also Mrs. Patterson, Maryam's friends, the robbers, and even Karl Smith, the leader of the Gang Bang who had fought with Adam.

"Oh well," she thought, "dreams never make sense." She snuggled down to try to go back to sleep.

A loud noise suddenly jolted Nadia to complete wakefulness. It sounded like a shot gun. Was it possible that the war had come to her neighborhood?

She sat up and strained her ears to hear more. She heard several voices outside, and they sounded similar to the voices in her dream.

However, now that she was awake, it did not sound like a spy chant. It sounded like the voices were saying "FIRE! FIRE!"

Nadia rubbed her eyes. Could this be another part of her dream?

She pinched herself. No, she was certainly awake. She looked out the window and could not see a thing except for thick smoke.

"Maryam, Eppa, wake up!" she screamed. "There's a fire!" Nadia scooped up the half asleep Eppa and ran toward the door.

Maryam, still sleepy, sat up slowly.

"Hurry up, we have to get out of here," Nadia urged her sister.

She opened the bedroom door. Flames were all around. By now Eppa was awake, and she began screaming as Nadia began to drag her towards the stairway yelling "HELP, FIRE!"

Maryam was now wide awake. "Get Eppa downstairs, I will go get the others," she commanded Nadia. The other two bedrooms were in front of the apartment.

"You will never get down that hallway," Nadia told her sister. Let's all get downstairs and call 911." She remembered what the firemen who visited their classroom had told them.

"Nadia, I can't go down there without the rest of the family," Maryam cried. "You call 911. I will crawl down the hall. Don't worry!"

Nadia watched as the image of her sister crawling faded into the smoke and flames. She did not have a good feeling about this, but she knew that there was not much she could say or do to convince Maryam to come with her.

"Come on Eppa," she said soothingly to her screaming little sister.

The two got down the stairs fairly easy. However, when they reached the bottom, Nadia was horrified to see that the entire front half of the store had already burned. There was no way she could get to the telephone!

She felt like panicking, but she knew from her emergency training in Iraq that panicking would not help. She knew that instead, she had to keep her head cool if there was any chance to save herself and her family.

She continued to push her way through the smoke. The hardest part was dragging Eppa, who didn't yet know the rule about not panicking. Eppa continued to scream, to struggle with Nadia, and to resist being pulled towards the door.

Nadia was moving quickly, but the fire was growing even faster. Soon she could no longer see the door, and had lost her sense of where the door even was. She dropped to her knees, continuing to pull her screaming sister by her arm.

"No, no, let Eppa go," her sister screamed.

By now, both girls were coughing from the smoke and burning from the heat, but the fire itself had not reached them yet. Nadia kept on going, hoping and praying that she was headed in the right direction. She was not sure, though, as she was very disoriented.

"Ouch!" She realized she had crawled into a large metal shelf and was unable to go forward any more. Now Nadia felt real panic setting in as the fire crept towards her from the other three sides.

She sat down to take a breath. She put her sister on her lap and began hugging her.

"Eppa, we must pray for a miracle," she told the baby. "We need a miracle to help us get out, and we need a miracle for our family to be saved."

Eppa did not hear a word Nadia said. She had stopped screaming and was instead sobbing deliriously. Even though she was only two, she seemed to know that this was a life and death situation.

"Dear Jesus, help us all get out safe and sound," Nadia prayed fervently. It was the only prayer she could think of, so she repeated it as she made the sign of the cross over and over again. The flames and smoke continued to engulf the girls.

Suddenly, in the middle of her prayer, Nadia had an idea. "Why not try to knock over the shelf and crawl over it?" she thought to herself. "Anything is better than just sitting here and burning to death."

She let go of her sobbing sister and stood up. She took a big step back and pushed forward on the shelf as hard as she could. It hobbled slightly.

She tried a second time, and this time the big metal structure hobbled more. She hoped that this wasn't one of the shelves that were up against the wall, but it was hard to tell.

She had no choice but to keep trying. This time she threw her entire body against the shelf with all of her might, saying a prayer as she did so.

"CRASH!" the shelf toppled and Nadia toppled with it. There was the sound of glass shattering, as if bottles had fallen and broken.

Nadia fell on top of the shelf and felt glass piercing her body. She could hear Eppa crying, but could not see a thing and did not even know where Eppa was anymore.

"Help, help!" she cried in despair. She did not have the strength to get up, and had no idea where she was.

"Please God, I'm too young to die!" was her last thought, as she drifted away in agony.

Chapter 7
Sweet Dreams

Nadia did not remember another thing until she woke up many hours later in an unfamiliar place. Where was she? What had happened to her? She was very confused and disoriented, and she ached all over.

Just then a nurse walked in. "Surprise, you are awake!" she exclaimed pleasantly. "I am Mrs. Geddes and will be taking care of you. How are you feeling?"

"I have a huge headache," Nadia replied. "I also feel sore all over. What happened and where am I? Where is my family?"

Mrs. Geddes smiled. "You are in Children's Hospital being treated for injuries you received in a fire," she replied. "Do you remember the fire?"

Nadia's heart raced. "I do remember the fire," she answered the nurse. "I thought I died, and I thought everyone in my family died, too."

She became anxious. "Where is my family? Are they all okay?"

"Nadia, your family is doing fine," the nurse replied. "You and Maryam were the only ones hurt, and Maryam was released right away. You are going to be in here for another day or two."

The nurse winked. “You and your sister are the heroes in this town for saving your family,” she said. “I will let your family tell you the whole story of what happened. Visiting hours begin shortly, and I know that some of your family will be here soon to see you.”

Nadia was still dazed and confused but was too weak to ask any more questions. She lay back down on the hospital bed.

“I will bring you some gelatin and juice. You should try to eat and begin to get your strength back,” Mrs. Geddes said. “I’ll be right back.”

As Nadia waited for her food and her family, she tried to remember the fire. It seemed to her like the whole thing was a bad nightmare, but she knew from her painful wounds that it had really happened.

The details all started coming back to her: the burning flames, the choking smoke, Eppa’s cries in the night, and finally that last horrible sound of breaking glass.

She looked down at her aching body, which had cuts and bandages all over. “I guess that part about all the glass breaking was not a dream,” she thought sadly.

By now she could not stop all the questions from swirling around crazily in her head. “How did everyone else get out?? How did the fire start? Where will we live? How will dad make his money now?” she wondered.

She was so tired and weak that she found herself sobbing. "Why had their wonderful life in America taken such a horrible turn this past month?" she asked herself. "First the robbery, then the bombing in New York, and now this!"

It was too much for her to bear.

Finally Mama and Maryam ended Nadia's self pity as they burst into the room.

"The nurse told us that you finally woke up," Maryam exclaimed. "We are so glad to see you awake. How are you feeling?"

Nadia shrugged through her tears. She didn't want her mother and sister to know how badly she felt. She knew they must also be upset about the fire.

"Pretty sore," she replied. "I thought I was dead, though. Where is everyone else? Please tell me the whole story of what happened."

"Eppa, Daniel and Father are at Uncle Mike's and Aunt Sheila's house," Mrs. Sefro replied to her first question. "That is where we are staying for now."

"Everyone is staying there except Adam and me," interrupted Maryam. "It is too far from our schools, so I am staying at Jane's house and Adam was invited to stay at the Johnson's."

Nadia was surprised that Adam was invited anywhere, but she was too emotionally exhausted to ask about it.

It turned out she didn't have to ask about Adam, or anything else for that matter. Mama and Maryam couldn't wait to explain to Nadia the entire story of what had happened that night.

There were many different parts of the story. The best part was that Nadia and Eppa had been saved by neighbors. The shelf that Nadia had knocked over had broken a window to the outdoors. The neighbors had heard the breaking glass and the girls' cries, and been able to rush in and rescue them.

"Kendra was one of the people who heard you and pointed her brother in the right direction to save you," Maryam informed her.

Nadia's heart raced. Her best friend had helped save her!! She thought they would never speak to each other again, but she was wrong. Kendra actually cared enough to help save Nadia's life! Nadia could not believe it.

"What about you?" Nadia asked. "How did you all get out?"

"I made it to mom and dad's room, but we could not get out the bedroom door. So we opened the windows and shouted as loud as we could."

Maryam laughed as she told the story. "I guess we were loud, because the firemen found us and climbed up to the window to save us. They were able to go back in and save Daniel and Adam, too. I was the only one who was hurt a little from crawling in the burning hallway to get to the other rooms."

Nadia's mind was racing even faster than her sister was talking. "What about all of our belongings?" she asked. "Will they be able to fix our house and our store so that we can live and work there again?"

The look on her mother's face told her the answer. "Nadia, we lost everything we owned," Mrs. Sefro replied gently. "However, this family has been through enough by now to know that money and things are not important. Just like with the robbery, it is most important that we are all safe and well."

"But mother, it's so unfair," Nadia collapsed deeper into the hospital bed. "Our family has had the worst luck in the whole entire world!

She continued. "First we lose our baby brother; then we have to move to America," she sobbed. "Then, all in one month we have a robbery, a fire, and our friends blaming us for the acts of war.

"When will our lives be nice and normal, like the lives of Americans?"

"Nadia, life is not fair," her mother sighed. "We should be grateful for tough situations, as they help make us into stronger people."

Mrs. Sefro brightened up as she suddenly remembered something she hadn't told Nadia yet.

"Nadia, life isn't all bad," she said." I should tell you two pieces of good news now so that you can think good thoughts before you fall back to sleep."

"Okay, momma, I need some good news," Nadia said.

"First of all, the police have found the people who have been causing us many of these problems," Mrs. Sefro explained. "Four people are now in jail."

Maryam interrupted her mother again. "They found out that it was Karl Smith and his Bang Gang who started the fire. They did it because they hate all people from the Middle East and blame them for the New York bombings."

She caught her breath. "While they were being questioned for the fire, two of them also admitted that they were the robbers that got away last month," she concluded.

She stopped to take a breath and Mrs. Sefro continued.

"I am very sad for those boys who threw their lives away due to how much hate they had in their hearts," she said. "We should always pray for them.

"However, I am happy that the neighborhood is safer with these boys behind bars. Also, maybe now Adam will have an easier time at school."

Nadia just lay quietly and listened to her sister and her mother tell their stories.

"There is more good news," said Maryam. "Here are some cards that the kids in your class made for you."

She opened her purse and pulled out a large bundle of envelopes.

"Your classmates are all very concerned about you and want you to get well soon," Mrs. Sefro explained gently. "They feel very badly for how they treated you. And now they understand that we are not connected with the terrorists."

"In fact," Maryam jumped in again, "Kendra said you can stay at her house once you are released from the hospital."

Nadia managed a small smile. The thought of staying with her friend warmed her heart.

"Could you please put the get well cards on the table? she asked. "I don't have the energy to read through them now."

She closed her eyes, which ached like the rest of her.

"I need to sleep, but I have one more question, Mother," she said weakly. "Where will we live now that our apartment is burned down? How will we afford to eat if we don't have the store any more?"

Mrs. Sefro patted her daughter's hand. "Don't worry, dear Nadia. I still have my job, and we have family and friends who are willing to help us," she said soothingly. "We will trust in our God to find us a way to get by, Nadia. He always has before."

Nadia smiled. Her mother was right. Nothing was more important then having family and friends who love you.

She quickly dozed back to sleep, but this time she would not have a single nightmare about spies, fires or robberies.

Instead, her dreams would be sweet dreams about loving family and caring friends.

Chapter 8
Rebuilding

Nadia could not believe that it was mid-November already. September and October had flown by quickly for all of the Sefro children.

These days, Nadia was staying with Kendra during the school weeks. On Fridays, Mr. Sefro would pick Nadia, Maryam, and Adam up from their friends' houses in Detroit and bring them back to their cousins' house for the weekends.

Nadia was happy and keeping busy with her school work, friends and cousins. However, she still felt anxious about their housing situation. She knew they could not live this way forever, but she didn't dare ask her parents what the plan was. She did not want to upset them or get in trouble for being rude.

As she sat there pondering her future, Adam bounced into the room. "Don't forget, tonight is Saturday," he said cheerfully. "We are all going back to the city for the special candlelight vigil."

Nadia could not believe how much happier her brother was now that the "Gang Bang" had been broken up. His happiness was also related to his stay with the Johnson family during the week. Jeff Johnson had become Adam's best friend, and he had introduced him to a lot of other nice friends from the middle school.

“I hear that the newly elected mayor will be at the vigil,” said Maryam. “He and Judge Boyd will both be speaking.”

“Mayor Kilpatrick is coming tonight?” Nadia was suddenly very interested. “What will they speak about?”

“It is going to be a peace rally so that everyone is inspired to work and live together in the city without violence or prejudice,” Maryam explained. “I can’t wait to hear what Judge Boyd has to say.”

“Personally, I am excited to hear our new mayor speak,” Adam said. “I hear he is young and hip, and he has a lot of great new ideas to help the city.

He continued. “Most of the kids in my class said they would be there. There is even a party after the rally.”

“My friends are all going to be there, too!” exclaimed Nadia excitedly. “This will be Hanna’s first chance to meet many of them.”

Hanna laughed. “I’ve heard enough about your friends. I feel like I already know them,” she said. “By the way, did anyone tell you guys that we are going to Detroit before the rally for a surprise?” Her eyes twinkled.

“What kind of surprise?” Nadia asked her cousin.

"I have no idea, but Mom and Dad told me that it was very special," Hanna responded. "We will find out soon enough. They told me we could leave as soon as Dad gets home, and I think he's coming now! Isn't that his van?"

"Of course it is. How many minivans are bright green with yellow letters saying 'Sefros' Fruit and Deli?'" Nadia laughed.

The children all hurried to get ready for the family trip into the city. "We will need to take two cars if everyone is going," said Aunt Sheila.

The children could not wait to see the surprise, so it didn't take long before both vehicles were full and ready to go.

The ride to Detroit seemed longer than normal. After what seemed like hours, the families turned down Palmer Lane, a beautiful tree lined street in Detroit with big old red brick houses.

"Oh, I know the surprise," blurted out Maryam. "The Sarofis had their new baby! I forgot about that! Was it a boy or girl? I can't wait to see it!"

"No, they haven't had the baby yet, Maryam," her mother replied. "You still haven't guessed the secret!"

The children all looked at one another in wonder until fMr. Sefro pulled up the driveway of the last brick house on the street.

"Ta da," said Mr. Sefro proudly. "Part of our big surprise is that we bought this house for our family to live in! What do you think, kids?"

The children all began talking at once as they scurried out of the van.

Nadia couldn't believe it! The house that father and mother had purchased was big, beautiful, had a huge yard and was still in the city!

"But father, I thought you wanted to move out to the suburbs near Uncle Mike," she said.

"Little girls should not be listening to adult conversations," her father said sternly. "When they don't know all of the facts, they can get the wrong ideas."

By now, the children were all buzzing excitedly. "Let's go take a grand tour," suggested Mrs. Sefro. "The house is officially ours, and right now it's vacant."

The new house had so many rooms that Nadia could not believe their good fortune. There were four large bedrooms instead of three small ones like they had at the tiny apartment. She and Eppa would share a large bedroom while Maryam got her very own room. Adam and Daniel would also share a bedroom.

There were also three large bathrooms in the new house as well as a huge kitchen, playroom and basement.

"How did we afford such a large house, Father?" Adam asked.

"Well, children, you helped us to earn this house," Mr. Sefro replied. "You have all worked hard so that mother could continue to work at her job."

He paused, and then continued. "Also, we received the insurance money for the store and the apartment."

"We received money for the store and apartment?" Nadia was confused. She thought they had lost everything they owned in the fire. Who would give them money for a burned down building?

"Insurance is a program to help people in case there are tragedies," Mrs. Sefro explained. "People pay money into an insurance fund, and the funds are given to people who are in the plan when they have a fire or an accident.

"We are very lucky that your uncle convinced us to purchase plenty of insurance for our building when we moved here," she smiled.

"Yes, and don't forget, Uncle Mike also convinced you to do something else."

Nadia giggled to hear her uncle talking about himself. "This new house is only part of the surprise," Uncle Mike said.

The children looked at one another. What more could there possibly be?

"Should I explain it, or do you want to?" Uncle Mike asked his brother.

"Let me explain it my way," replied Nadia's father, "because I have some very important points I want to talk about. Let's all go out in the new backyard and sit down on our new deck so that we can discuss the plan in detail."

The families all ran to the back deck where Aunt Sheila had just finished setting up a surprise: a beautiful picnic dinner! She had spread several large blankets all around. The blankets contained plates of fried chicken, potato salad and all types of bread and fruit from their store.

"This is an American picnic," Aunt Sheila laughed.

"My favorite kind!" Adam yelled. "I'm starving."

While they ate the delicious dinner, Mr. Sefro outlined the new plan.

"We are going to rebuild our store differently," he explained. "Uncle Mike will be my partner, and he has helped me draw up some plans."

"We have sold the property where our party store was, and we purchased the old grocery store on Six Mile Road," Mr.

Sefro continued. "They will begin fixing up the store this week, and it should be finished in time for the Christmas season."

He continued with his good news. "We will keep selling everything that we sell now, so that we can keep our current customers happy. However, we will also grow lots of produce in our new garden to sell at the store, and we will offer breads and many other grocery items as well."

All of the children started asking questions at once, but Mr. Sefro put up his hand to silence them. "Please wait until we finish," he commanded, "and then ask your questions. Would you like to explain why we are doing this?" he turned to his wife.

Mrs. Sefro smiled at her husband and continued his story. "We thought we wanted to move into the suburbs, away from all of the big city problems," she said. "However, we know how much you are all feeling at home in Detroit. The city is improving every day, and most of the people who live here are very good people.

"We are proud of how our own children have learned not to be prejudiced," continued Nadia's mother. "We have decided that we want to stay in the city of Detroit and help rebuild it."

"We also feel that we can not always run away from problems," Mr. Sefro added. "We felt we had no choice but to move from Iraq. However, we feel that here in Detroit, we have the chance to stay and help solve the problems."

There was a long silence. The subject had become so serious! Mr. Sefro seemed to be finished, but no one dared to interrupt until they were sure.

Aunt Sheila finally broke the silence. “What does everyone think about the new house and the plans for the new store?” she asked.

“I LOVE THE NEW PLANS!” Nadia found herself shouting loudly. She just couldn’t help it.

“Eppa love it too,” Eppa yelled.

“Yes, yes, yes!” Maryam added her opinion louder than Nadia had ever heard her speak.

Soon all of the children joined in the whooping and hollering, jumping up and down and giving each other American high fives.

Nadia finally stopped yelling enough to go hug her parents. “This is the best surprise I could have ever dreamed about,” she told them happily. “Thank you, mother and father.”

The other kids joined in. “Thank you, thank you!!” they yelled.

“Tank you, this best surprise Eppa ever dream about,” Eppa said.

“You said it, baby!” laughed Maryam.

The oldest sister suddenly became serious as she said the words that Nadia had been thinking.

“Our family has been through a lot, but we stick together and we are strong,” Maryam explained to baby Eppa.

"You will learn soon, baby, that we have the best family and friends, and the best life in the whole world.”

About the Author

Donna Gundle-Krieg lives in Milford, Michigan, with her husband Dennis, their children Steven and Elizabeth, dog Becka, cat Sombrita, and birds Misty and Whistler.

Donna has been published in a variety of books and publications. Recently published articles address adoption, bullying, education, gun control, human resource management, and gardening. Samples of these articles can be found at www.blitzkriegpublishing.com.

Over the years, she has had a variety of diverse experiences including managing restaurants and retail stores, and working as a human resources consultant. She is also a certified Master Gardener.

In addition, Donna has home schooled one or more of her children for several years and is very involved in the local home schooling movement. As a member of the "Million Mom March," she has a special interest in bullying, and is dedicated to helping children understand that peace and understanding are the only answer.

To contact Donna, email her at dokrieg@comcast.net or visit the blitzkriegpublishing.com website.

Printed in the United States
19993LVS00001B/379-441